L⊙ST

IN THE SEA OF DESPAIR

WARNING!

The instructions in this book are for extreme survival situations only and are not intended for use as a guide on sailing trips. Always proceed with caution, and ask an adult to supervise – or, ideally, seek professional help. If in doubt, consult a responsible adult.

Published 2014 by
A & C Black, an imprint of
Bloomsbury Publishing Plc
50 Bedford Square, London, WC1B 3DP

www.bloomsbury.com

Bloomsbury is a registered trademark of Bloomsbury Publishing Plc

978-1-4729-0622-9

Text copyright © 2014 Tracey Turner
Illustration copyright © 2014 Nelson Evergreen
Copyright © 2014 A & C Black
Additional images © Shutterstock

Printed by CPI Group (UK) Ltd, Croydon CR0 4YY

1 3 5 7 9 10 8 6 4 2

MIX
Paper from
responsible sources
FSC® C020471

LOST

IN THE SEA OF DESPAIR

TRACEY TURNER

A & C BLACK
AN IMPRINT OF BLOOMSBURY
LONDON NEW DELHI NEW YORK SYDNEY

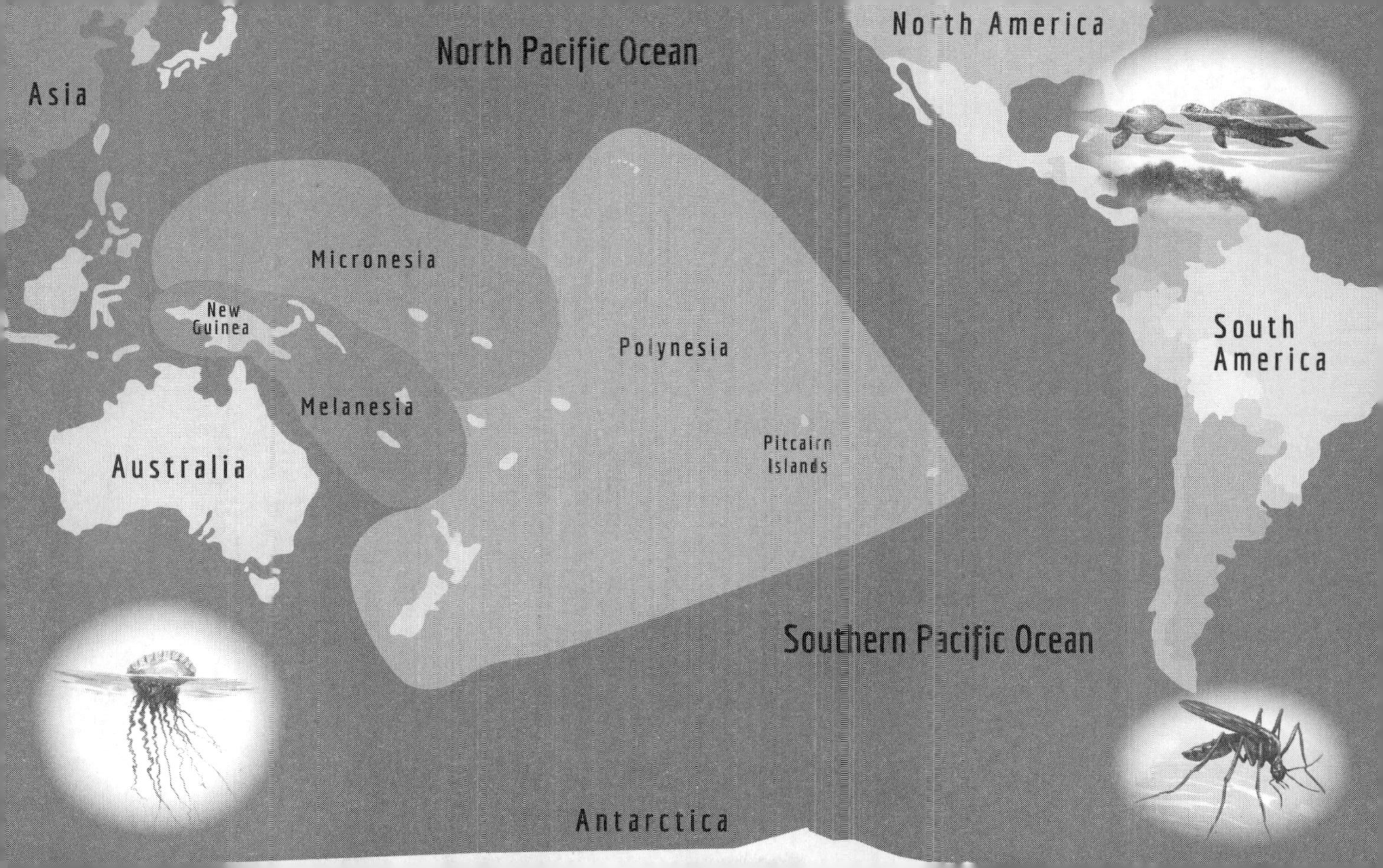
North Pacific Ocean
Asia
North America
Micronesia
New Guinea
Polynesia
South America
Melanesia
Australia
Pitcairn Islands
Southern Pacific Ocean
Antarctica

Welcome to your adventure!
STOP! Read this first!

Welcome to an action-packed adventure in which you take the starring role!

You're about to become lost at sea in the vast Pacific Ocean, battling against towering waves, raging storms, and deadly sharks. On each page choose from different options – according to your instincts, knowledge and intelligence – and navigate your own way to safety.

You decide . . .
- How to spot a venomous shellfish
- What to do when you're surrounded by hungry hammerhead sharks
- How to find food on a desert island

. . . and many more life-or-death dilemmas. Along the way you'll discover the facts you need to help you survive.

It's time to test your survival skills – or die trying!

Your adventure starts on page 7.

You watch helplessly as the small orange life raft bobs out of sight in the churning waves. You clutch the rail of the yacht as another massive wave crashes over you, wondering how on Earth you're going to survive.

Tonight's terrible events swirl around your head like a nightmare. Your uncle woke you up when he discovered the small yacht was letting in water from a hole in the hull. It was the middle of the night, with a storm raging around you – so different from when you'd set off on this trip, sailing into the South Pacific on a calm, sunny day. Trying to repair the hole, your uncle got washed overboard. He shouted for you to throw him a life raft. You saw him inflate it and climb into it, just before the tiny raft got lost among gigantic waves.

Your uncle is an experienced sailor, but you have no knowledge of sailing at all. Yet here you are, far from land, surrounded by crashing waves, in a leaking boat. The yacht pitches and rolls, nearly hurling you into the sea. You are lost in the Pacific, and completely alone.

How will you survive?

Turn to page 8 to find information you need to help you survive.

The Pacific is vast. The largest of the world's oceans, it covers roughly 28% of the Earth's surface, stretching from the Arctic in the north to the waters of the Antarctic in the south. To the west, the Pacific is bounded by Asia and Australia, and to the east by North and South America.

You are lost in the tropical South Pacific. The sea here is dotted with islands, and you might be lucky enough to find one – but there is a lot more sea than land: the islands of the South Pacific are some of the most remote in the world, scattered over 31,000 square kilometres. Many people have become lost in the Pacific Ocean, never to return. If you're going to survive you'll need to have your wits about you.

Perils of the South Pacific

The open sea is probably the most challenging survival environment of all. No one can survive in cold water for very long, but here in the tropics you stand a much better chance of staying alive. As well as the perils of surviving on a tiny boat in a huge sea, you will have to contend with brutal tropical storms, sharks, whales and other large marine mammals, which could capsize your craft. Closer to shore, jellyfish, sea snakes, stingrays and other venomous sea creatures might be lurking. If you do find land, you need to beware of fatal diseases such as malaria, and be wary of any creatures you might meet.

Island Life

There are thousands of islands in the South Pacific, divided geographically into Micronesia, Melanesia and Polynesia. The largest island is New Guinea, which covers nearly 700,000 square kilometres, while the smallest inhabited island is Pitcairn, just five square kilometres. There are thousands of uninhabited islands too, some much smaller than Pitcairn. Often, the reason an island is uninhabited is because there's no fresh water available. The islands vary dramatically – there are different cultures and languages, wildlife and plant life. Generally speaking, the further west, the more plants and animals you'll find. Further east there are fewer species.

Turn to page 10.

Basic Survival Tips at Sea

Here are a few basic tips that might affect your chances of survival at sea . . .

- On board any boat, find out where life rafts, life belts and lifejackets are, and make sure you're familiar with emergency drills.

- Stay with the boat for as long as possible before abandoning it for a life raft – it will have more supplies on board and be easier for rescuers to spot.

- If you can, let Search and Rescue services know you are abandoning your boat for a life raft.

- If a call for help has been successfully sent, stay in the same position (life rafts have sea anchors that stop them from drifting). If a call hasn't been sent, keep the raft moving.

- Make sure you're protected from the elements as much as possible.

- Drinking water is a priority – if you don't have a desalinator (see page 23), find ways to collect rain or make a solar still (see page 45). Never drink seawater.

- Take deep breaths and stay calm. Panicking will seriously reduce your chances of survival.

Remember this book is not intended as an official guide to sailing trips.

Turn to page 11.

The storm is dying down a bit, but the little yacht is still pitching wildly from side to side.

The hole in the side of the hull is still letting in water, and now that you can move about more easily and safely you open the door to the cabin and start bailing the water out over the side with a bucket. You're bailing faster than the water's coming in, but you wonder how long you can keep this up.

There's a second life raft – you spotted it when you picked up the first one, and your uncle shouted to you that you might need to use it. Maybe it would be better to abandon the boat now, and set off in the other life raft?

If you decide to abandon ship, go to page 36.

If you decide to stay with the yacht, go to page 20.

By choosing to inflate the life raft on the side of the listing hull, which is also the windward side of the yacht, you're going to make life very difficult for yourself. Not only will you have to jump down into it with the wind blowing in your face, but the life raft risks becoming ripped on the barnacles that cling to the bottom of the boat.

In the first glimmer of dawn light, you throw the raft over the side. You follow the instructions on the outside of the life raft's canister, pulling on a long chord to make it inflate. Just when you're starting to think there must be something wrong with it, the life raft pops open with a loud hissing noise. The raft inflates, its canopy pops up automatically, and you jump down into it over the side of the yacht's hull. Now you have to push the life raft away from the yacht. But before you have a chance to do this, a wave smashes the raft into the hull.

Your blood freezes as you hear an ominous ripping sound, then air hissing out of the raft. Panic-stricken, you consider trying to get back onto the boat, abandoning the raft. If it's torn, how long can it last? But, luckily for you, there's secondary inflation on this life raft and you hear it inflating automatically. Phew.

Go to page 15.

You take out the paddle and splash it down on the surface of the waves. The turtle doesn't seem to notice. You feel another bump underneath the raft – it's another turtle! Looking at the barnacles clinging to the turtles' rough shells, you reckon it's only a matter of time before they scrape and tear the bottom of the raft. You bash the paddle right next to the head of one of the turtles. Alarmed, it begins to swim away. The other one follows it.

You're relieved. You're checking underneath the raft, peering down into the blue sea, when the sun slips out from behind a cloud and you're able to see more clearly. But what you see makes the hairs on the back of your neck stand on end. Your heart races: underneath the raft are the unmistakable shapes of five large hammerhead sharks.

It worked with the turtles: maybe you should slap the water with the paddle to drive away the sharks, too?

If you decide to use the paddle to drive away the sharks, go to page 74.

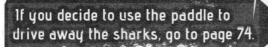

If you decide not to, go to page 30.

After a while, the raft starts to lurch sickeningly from side to side. You think the sea is getting rougher again, and you zip up the raft's canopy, grimly accepting the prospect of another storm on its way.

You were starting to feel sick anyway, and now that you can't see outside the raft you feel an awful lot worse. You put your hands over your mouth and concentrate hard on not being sick. But it's no good – in a rush, you unzip the canopy, stick your head out and vomit into the sea.

You lie down, feeling terrible, and take some seasickness pills.

Go to page 32.

The little life raft bobs along on its precarious way. You hope that you'll be rescued, or find land, before anything else has a chance to tear the raft – you've used up your secondary inflation before you've even started.

You're unlucky, though. The raft comes supplied with a sharp knife, and you take it out of its sheath to have a look at it. You drop it, point first onto your inflated raft. It pierces the raft, in just the place the barnacles ripped a hole earlier.

You scrabble for the raft's repair kit. You're panicking, but you manage to stick on a patch, and bail out the water that's leaked in. The patch doesn't last very long, though – you can't bail fast enough and, inevitably, the raft starts to take in more and more water, until it sinks, taking you with it.

The end.

The boat has completely over turned now, and you climb up on top of the hull. The sun has come up, and you scan the sky for a helpful plane or helicopter. But there's nothing but heavy, grey clouds in the sky, and nothing on the horizon except white-topped waves.

Go to page 24.

The turtles must be interested in your raft, because they keep swimming underneath it, from one side to the other. Maybe they're finding something to eat there. Whatever the reason, you become increasingly worried about the turtles' hard shells rubbing against the bottom of the raft.

You're right to be worried: the turtles have worn away at the raft's strong fabric. As one of the turtles disappears underneath the raft for what seems like the hundredth time, you hear the bottom of the raft tear. Your heart pounds: the air is hissing out of one section of the life raft's buoyant air compartments! Luckily, though, the life raft has a secondary buoyancy layer – there's no need to attempt a repair. At least, not for now.

The turtles seem to have swum away, but you're going to try and frighten them away if they come back – there aren't any more chances if they damage the raft again.

Go to page 38.

Unfortunately, splashing the surface of the sea doesn't alarm the sharks at all. In fact, it makes them more curious – the predators are attracted to splashing in case it's a fish thrashing about near the surface. This is exactly the kind of thing sharks' primitive brains are attuned to seek out.

The sharks become so interested that they take a bite out of the paddle to find out what it is . . . then the raft. . . and then you.

The end.

Hammerhead Sharks

- The strange shape of the hammerhead's head is thought to help them find their prey more easily: their eyes are wide-set, and their heads also contain special organs that sense other creatures, so they can see and sense a wide area.

- Hammerheads prey on fish, shellfish, octopus, squid, and their favourite food, stingrays. Their special sensory organs help them find the stingrays even when they're buried under sand. They use their hammerheads to pin stingrays to the sea floor as they attack.

- There are different species of hammerhead. Most types are quite small and not usually dangerous to people. The largest, the great hammerhead, can grow up to six metres long – this is the type you've just encountered.

- Hammerheads are found all over the world, in both tropical and cooler seas, and both close to land and far out at sea.

The storm has died down even more and you keep bailing out the water coming in through the hole. As the first light of dawn appears, the full horror of your predicament becomes clear: the yacht is obviously sinking, it's only matter of time before it goes under, no matter how quickly you bail, and you're already exhausted. You take a look at the waterlogged radio, flicking the switches on and off, but there's no sign of life.

It looks as though it's time to inflate the life raft. But maybe you'd be better off staying with the yacht? After all, it's much bigger and easier to spot than a little raft.

If you decide to stay with the sinking boat, go to page 16.

If you decide to inflate the life raft, go to page 36.

Abandoning Ship

It's a good idea to stay with a boat or ship until the point of no return – it's easier for rescuers to see than a life raft, and there are more things in it that can help you survive. But once that point has been reached, there's nothing for it but to abandon ship . . .

- Stay calm! Panic will lead to bad decisions.

- If you can, make distress calls.

- If the shore or other ships are nearby, fire distress flares.

- Put on extra clothes – keep as warm as you can – and a life jacket.

- Take seasickness tablets.

- Find the Emergency Grab Bag (see page 23).

- Prepare to launch the life raft (see page 37).

You throw the life raft over the side, which is now listing close to the surface of the sea. The raft comes in a canister, and there are instructions telling you to pull out a long rope to its fullest extent, then give it a sharp tug. As you give the final tug, the raft inflates by itself with a loud hiss as gas rushes into the raft's inflatable chambers. You'd be impressed if you weren't so terrified.

Just before you jump into the raft, abandoning the yacht, you spot something else that might help – fixed next to the wheel you spot a large bag labelled Emergency Grab Bag.

You investigate the raft and the Grab Bag. Among other things, you notice seasickness pills and sick bags. You feel OK at the moment, but maybe you should take some pills to be on the safe side?

If you decide to take seasickness pills, go to page 32.

If you decide not to, go to page 14.

Emergency Grab Bag

There are lots of useful things in the life raft, but the Grab Bag contains some life-saving extras:

- The most important object is a desalinator – operated by a hand pump, the desalinator makes seawater drinkable if you follow the instructions. You can make about a litre of drinkable water an hour – more than enough to allow you to survive. If it weren't for the desalinator, you'd have to make a solar still, collect rainwater, or water that's condensed inside the raft.

Other useful items include:

- A small waterproof bag of toiletries, including a toothbrush, toothpaste, sunscreen and lip balm.

- Dry clothing and lightweight thermal blankets in a waterproof bag, including a sun hat and sunglasses.

- A pack of cards.

- Extra seasickness pills and sick bags (there are some already in the life raft).

- Matches in a waterproof container.

The sea is getting rougher. You begin to realise that you've been foolish to stay with the yacht instead of inflating the life raft. You can't reach anything that can help you survive, whereas inside the life raft there are all sorts of useful things. But it's impossible to get to it now.

Things get worse: water must have reached a vital chamber inside the yacht, because one end of it slumps downwards. The boat is starting to sink.

After the boat has sunk, you cling to some cushions that have floated to the surface. Eventually they start to sink too. You soon become exhausted and cold. You drown.

The end.

Open Sea Survival

- You will only be able to survive in cold water for a short time before hypothermia sets in – depending on the temperature, this could be a matter of minutes.

- In very cold water, people go into shock straight away, breathing uncontrollably fast and deep – this lasts about three minutes. If someone goes under the water during that time, they swallow water and drown. After about three minutes, people can survive in temperatures of five degrees Celsius for up to about 20 minutes.

- Water drains heat from the body much faster than air. The more of a person's body that's underwater, the faster they will cool down, so if you can find something to float on you will be better off.

- Even water temperatures as high as 27 degrees Celsius can be dangerous – heat will still be lost from the body, though people will survive much longer before they lose heat and become hypothermic.

- If you find yourself awaiting rescue submerged in water and can't climb onto something floating, keep your arms and legs in close to avoid losing heat. This will be difficult unless you have a life jacket.

You slowly and carefully edge towards the bird, hanging on to the outside of the raft. It cocks its head to one side, staring at you with a beady eye, but it doesn't look alarmed. You inch closer. It's almost within your grasp. Just a bit further and you'll be able to grab the bird's legs . . .

You lunge for the creature, which takes off with a loud squawk of alarm, you slip on the outside of the raft and plunge into the sea. A wave carries you away from the raft. You struggle in the water to get back to it, but the distance between you and the raft becomes greater and greater.

You bitterly regret trying to catch the bird. It's your final thought before you become too tired to carry on swimming, and drown.

The end.

Pacific Sea Birds

- Red-footed and brown boobies are the two species of booby likely to be found in the South Pacific – the bird you tried to catch is a red-footed booby. Blue-footed boobies live in the Galapagos Islands and the Pacific coasts of North and South America.

- Red-footed boobies live in the Atlantic, Pacific and Indian Oceans, and often land on boats. They nest on land, but can fly up to 150 kilometres looking for food – usually fish or squid – and can dive as deep as 30 metres after prey.

- As well as boobies, noddies are found in the South Pacific, especially brown noddies, which also live in the Caribbean, the Red Sea and the Indian Ocean, and blue noddies, which nest on islands in the South Pacific.

- You might also spot great frigatebirds, which sometimes chase other birds to get them to drop or regurgitate their fish. Males have a red pouch in their throats that they inflate like a balloon to attract female frigatebirds.

- Watch which way birds fly in the evening – they are heading in the direction of land.

You spend a sleepless night, tossing and turning and wondering what that bump was. Every so often you feel something else nudge the bottom of the boat. You desperately want to go to sleep and forget about it – even if you knew what was making the bumps, what could you do about it? Finally, you manage to drift off into a fitful sleep for a few hours.

Go to page 54.

Whales and Dolphins

The South Pacific is home to different species of whales and dolphins, some of which you might meet, because they're curious animals. The bumps you felt were made by curious bottlenose dolphins. Here are a few species of whales and dolphins that live in the South Pacific . . .

- Bottlenose and spinner dolphins are the marine acrobats of the South Pacific, performing amazing leaps and (as the spinner dolphin's name suggests), spins. They can reach speeds of up to 30 kilometres per hour. Dolphins of different species sometimes come together to form enormous pods of a thousand or more animals.

- Huge humpback whales can be up to 20 metres long, and could easily overturn a raft with a flick of their tail. Tonga in the South Pacific is a breeding ground for humpback whales.

- Pilot whales are usually found in deeper water in pods of between 10 and 30. William Butler (see page 118) blamed a pod of pilot whales for sinking his yacht in the Pacific.

Every so often, you peer outside of the raft. The menacing, unmistakable shapes are still there. There are more of them than you thought – you count nine. You decide not to look, and try to concentrate instead on a game of patience with your pack of cards, hoping that the creatures will get bored and go away.

Eventually, after an hour or two worrying about the hammerheads, you risk another look into the sea. They've gone! They must have caught the scent of something more interesting in the water. (To find out more about hammerhead sharks, go to page 19.)

You're starting to wonder when you'll spot another yacht or a ship, or maybe even an island. You unzip the raft and take a good look around. The sun is shining in a clear blue sky – no sign of a plane. Suddenly a dark shape in the water catches your eye. You very much wish it hadn't. It's huge – a three-metre-long creature, just a few metres below the surface and ten or so metres away from the raft. As the raft moves, blown by the wind and pushed by currents, the creature moves with it. You can clearly see by its shape that the creature is a huge shark, with a rounded, white-tipped dorsal fin, and it's following you.

Go to page 43.

Oceanic Whitetip Shark

The shark that's following your raft is an Oceanic Whitetip, considered to be one of the most dangerous sharks to humans.

- Oceanic Whitetips live out in open sea, in warmer waters, and are rarely seen close to land.

- Whitetips are usually solitary fish, but sometimes group together in a feeding frenzy if there's an opportunity for a good meal, such as a dead whale.

- These sharks aren't fussy about what they eat – fish, turtles, seabirds, octopus, crabs, dead whales and dolphins. They have extremely powerful jaws.

- Whitetips can be aggressive towards other sharks, and are also dangerous to people, though they rarely come into contact with people because of where they live.

- During the Second World War, it's thought that Oceanic Whitetips were responsible for the deaths of many survivors from ships sunk by torpedoes and bombs in tropical seas.

- Whitetips are curious and show no fear of divers – another reason they're considered highly dangerous.

- Whitetips can measure up to about four metres long, though most are smaller. There are other much bigger sharks, such as Great Whites, which reach up to about 6.5 metres.

Rain lashes the raft, the wind howls, and worst of all, huge waves send the raft plummeting down into deep troughs, and then carry it back up again in a terrible rollercoaster ride. In fact it's a hundred times worse than the most stomach-lurching theme-park ride you've ever been on.

Every time you feel the raft climbing an impossibly tall wave, you think it's going to overturn and sink on the way down – but it doesn't, the raft always rights itself. You brace yourself, clinging on to the raft's hand-holds, as the storm hurls you about.

Go to page 44.

Pacific Storms

- Storms in which the winds reach speeds of more than 118 kilometres per hour are classed as typhoons.

- Hurricanes, typhoons and cyclones are all the same type of weather, but the names are used in different areas: in the Atlantic and northeast Pacific it's a hurricane; in the northwest Pacific it's a typhoon; and in the South Pacific and Indian Ocean it's a cyclone.

- These violent storms are caused by warm air rising quickly, then getting pushed aside as it cools, causing it to spin.

- Cyclones, hurricanes and typhoons are identified by names. The first storm of the year is given a name beginning with A, the next beginning with B, and so on. If a storm does a lot of damage, that name is never used again.

- The tropical cyclone season in the South Pacific runs from November to April.

The storm is finally over. The sea calms, until the raft is rocking gently on the waves. It's an enormous relief not to feel yourself being hurled about the ocean, and gradually you stop feeling sick.

You're drifting, enjoying the relative comfort, when something bumps the bottom of the raft. Quickly, you unzip the canopy and look out. You can't see anything. Maybe it was a piece of driftwood. You feel another bump, quite strong this time. Watery sunlight is making its way through the grey clouds, and you make out a round shape emerging from underneath the raft. It's a turtle! The creature surfaces.

It's quite big – almost a metre long, you reckon – with a reddish-brown shell covered in barnacles. It could rip the life raft if it carries on bumping you from underneath – maybe you should try to frighten it away?

If you decide to frighten off the turtle, go to page 13.

If you decide to leave the creature alone, go to page 17.

Turtles

- Several different types of turtle live in the Pacific Ocean: green sea turtles, Pacific black sea turtles, hawksbill, leatherback, and loggerhead.

- Green sea turtles, which you've just encountered, are the largest hard-shelled turtles – their shells can reach 1.5 metres in diameter (the turtles are named for the colour of their skin not their shell). Loggerhead turtles' shells measure up to about a metre.

- The largest turtles of all are leatherbacks – they have soft shells which can measure two metres long. The largest one ever recorded measured 2.6 metres long, and weighed over 900 kilograms.

- Turtles lay their eggs on sandy beaches, but travel hundreds of kilometres out to sea. Female turtles often return to the beach were they were hatched to lay their own eggs.

- Turtles are carnivores. They eat jellyfish (which they sometimes mistake for plastic carrier bags), crabs and other shellfish, and fish. Occasionally they eat seaweed as well.

- Turtles feature in the myths and legends of Pacific Island people. They used to be a sacred food, which only nobles were allowed to eat.

You pull the life raft canister off the wall and try to make sense of it. You force yourself to breathe slowly and stop panicking – you know that you won't be able to work it out if you don't calm down. Taking deep breaths, you read the instructions on the outside. It inflates automatically – apparently you have to throw the canister into the sea, hanging on to a rope sticking out of one side, then pull the rope. You can't believe it's going to work.

The hole in the yacht has let in more water while you've been trying to work out the life raft instructions, and the yacht's now listing over to the side. Where should you launch the life raft? On the side closest to the water? Or should you throw the raft over the other side of the boat, next to the yacht's exposed hull?

If you decide to launch the raft on the side nearest the water, go to page 22.

If you decide to launch it on the other side, near the yacht's hull, go to page 12.

Life Rafts

There are different types of life raft. Some come in hard canisters, and inflate automatically – thankfully you have one of these, and it's a good one.

- The raft has a high-visibility canopy arch that covers the whole raft and inflates automatically. It has a door that zips open and closed.

- There are two buoyancy compartments – if one gets a hole in it, the other one takes over.

- The raft should be able to keep you alive for at least 30 days.

- The life raft comes equipped with various items to help you survive: a bailer, paddles, a knife, a mirror for signalling, a torch, a horn and a whistle for making noise that's more likely to be heard than shouting, a compass, a first-aid kit, sponges, flares, seasickness pills and sick bags, bellows (to top up the inflatable compartments of the raft), a fishing line and hook, and a repair kit.

You try to make yourself comfortable. Who knows how long it will be before you're rescued?

You arrange the waterproof bag of clothes as a pillow, and spread out the blankets underneath you. You're feeling much calmer now. You're also feeling hungry. There's one obvious source of food, and you're completely surrounded by it. Should you try your hand at fishing? You think you saw a fishing line in the life raft pack.

If you decide to fish, go to page 46.

If you decide not to, go to page 42.

Fishing

- The tropical waters of the South Pacific are teeming with life. Fish that you catch in the open sea should be safe to eat. However, any fish you catch that live in shallower waters close to land could be poisonous, so be careful.

- Most fish that's just been caught is safe to eat raw.

- You might even find that flying fish leap into your life raft without you having to catch them!

- When you're fishing, don't handle the fishing line with bare hands because it can be very sharp, especially when sea salt sticks to it. A fishing line could also damage the life raft.

- You'll have to go about the messy business of gutting any fish you catch. Cut any fish you don't eat straight away into thin strips and hang them up to dry – that way they may stay safe to eat for a day or two. Any fish you don't gut immediately will go bad quickly.

- You could also catch and eat turtles, though this could be greusome and difficult and you risk damaging the raft.

You gather up some dry grass, and make piles of twigs and some bigger pieces of driftwood. There's a breeze blowing, so you dig a hole and line it with stones as a fire pit. Soon you have a cheerful fire burning. There's no shortage of fuel for making fires here – you'll be warm and dry, and able to cook food.

At the thought of food, your stomach rumbles. You could go to the sea shore and fish. On the other hand, you think you might have spotted a much easier source of protein: there are lots of fat crickets hopping about at the edge of the forest, and you know that people eat insects in many different parts of the world. They're easy to catch, and all around you.

If you decide to go fishing, go to page 80.

If you decide to catch some insects, go to page 90.

Making a Fire

- Before you start, gather together everything you'll need: a prepared fireplace, matches, tinder (dry, flammable material), kindling (dry twigs and small branches) and fuel (larger branches).

- Choose a dry, sheltered spot to make your fire.

- Set your tinder alight – good **tinder** will only need a spark to light it.

- Build your kindling around the tinder in a pyramid.

- Gradually add larger pieces of wood, taking care not to add anything too big or too wet in the early stages of the fire, or you'll put it out.

- If there are stones available, you could use them to surround the fire, or even to line a fire pit. The stones will heat up and give off heat after the fire has gone out, and they'll also stop the fire from spreading out of control. But be careful not to use wet stones, especially ones that have been submerged in water, which can explode!

You're not hungry enough to try fishing just yet – and, anyway, you worry that you might be in danger of piercing the raft if you tried fishing with a hook.

But you do wonder what fish might be lurking down there, if any. You take a look over the side, and instantly wish you hadn't. Circling underneath your raft you can see a group of hammerhead sharks.

Go to page 30.

After a while of not daring to look, you peer out of the raft. The menacing dark shape is still there. You know that there is absolutely nothing you can do against a creature of this size and power: if it decides that your raft is prey, you'll just have to hope it's all over quickly.

A few hours later, the sun is beginning to sink beneath the horizon. You've heard sharks are more likely to feed at dusk and dawn. You gulp, take a deep breath, and have another look for the shark. You can't see it! You make another careful check – it's definitely gone! You almost cry with relief.

Something bashes against the top of the raft. What could it be? You're almost too frightened to look, but when you do you discover a friendly looking seabird with red webbed feet sitting on the top of your raft, having a rest.

It occurs to you that you could probably grab the bird quite easily and wring its neck. You need to eat to stay strong – if you allow yourself to become weak, your chances of survival are not good.

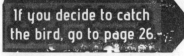

If you decide to catch the bird, go to page 26.

If you decide not to, go to page 48.

The storm dies down. The rain has stopped hammering on the raft's canopy, and you're not being hurled about nearly as much, though the waves are still big.

You're thirsty, and look in the Emergency Grab Bag for something to drink. There's a bottle of water, and you take a grateful swig. But there's also a desalinator – a machine that removes salt from seawater, making it drinkable.

You follow the instructions on the desalinator, and use its hand pump to pump seawater through a special filter, which removes almost all the salt. It's quite hard work, and you make a mental note not to use it when it's very hot. You're glad the desalinator was inside the Grab Bag – you won't have to worry about finding enough fresh water to survive.

Go to page 34.

Finding Water at Sea

You need water to live. Without it, you'll die in a few days. Luckily, you have your desalinator to provide drinkable water, but if you didn't have it on board your raft, you'd have to find other ways of obtaining drinkable water:

- Collect rainwater in containers. Some life rafts collect rainwater and funnel it into a pouch on the inside of the raft's canopy. Drink rainwater first, because any water you have in bottles will last for longer.

- Inflatable solar stills are sometimes included with life rafts. You fill the bottom of the still with seawater and attach it to the side of the raft. The salt water evaporates in the sun and drinkable water condenses on the inside and runs into a bottle. Solar stills are not much use in rough seas, because the salt water sloshes about and gets into the condensed water. You can also make your own solar still.

- Whatever you do, don't drink seawater – you might die more quickly than if you drink nothing at all. During the Second World War, some of the survivors from the *USS Indianapolis* drank seawater, began to imagine things and drowned as a result.

You use the hook and line in your survival pack, casting the hook away from the raft. You sit and wait. Nothing happens – but since you don't have any bait, maybe it's not surprising. You haul in the line so that you can attach something to the hook that might prove interesting to fish.

But disaster strikes. The hook has embedded itself in the bottom of the raft, and as you pull in the line, it rips a jagged hole – right where the turtle ripped the raft earlier on.

Before you've had a chance to do anything, the raft begins to sink. It's not long before you tire and drown.

The end.

The ship looks too far away to spot a flare. It's better to wait for a closer ship, or a plane, that has more of a chance of seeing you. That is, if you ever see another ship, you think dejectedly.

Over the next couple of weeks living on the island, you don't see any other sign of human life whatsoever.

Go to page 95.

You prepare for your first night aboard the raft. It doesn't seem possible that just 24 hours ago everything was fine – you were on board a sturdy yacht, with an experienced sailor and fully functioning radio equipment. Another bird comes to land on your raft, making you jump. You're glad it's nothing to be frightened of, and try to make yourself as comfortable as you can as darkness falls.

Go to page 58.

Signs of Land

There are lots of different signs that land might be nearby – watch out for them:

- Cumulus cloud – the fluffy, candyfloss kind – is often found hovering over or near an island. If the cloud has a flat bottom, that's an even better sign that land is close by.

- More birds are found near land than in the middle of the sea. Notice which way birds fly at dusk – they might be flying towards land to roost. At dawn, they will probably be flying from the direction of land.

- Lighter coloured water means that it's shallower, which could indicate that land is near.

- Look out for a greenish tinge in the sky in tropical seas – it might mean that sunlight's being reflected from a shallow lagoon.

- Sniff the air – you might smell muddy swamps.

- Listen out for the roar of surf on a beach.

Sure enough, you can feel that there's an animal inside the shell. It should make a tasty meal. But as you tap the shell to try and remove the shellfish, an agonising pain shoots up your arm.

You've been bitten by a cone shell. It's quite a big one, and its venom is highly toxic. You're in extreme pain, and your hand and arm swell up. You feel sick, and your muscles become paralysed. Eventually you stop breathing and die.

The end.

Cone Shells

- Cone shells are sea snails, and there are various different types. The larger ones – which can grow up to about 20 centimetres long – can be extremely venomous, while the smaller species have stings that aren't dangerous to people.

- Cone shells inject venom through a sharp, harpoon-like tooth that's strong enough to pierce the shells of other shellfish.

- Cone shells live throughout tropical waters, and live on worms, shellfish and small fish. The species that live on fish are the most dangerous – they need fast-acting poison to stop fish from swimming away.

- Cone shells are often brightly coloured and patterned, but don't be tempted to pick one up unless you're sure the shell is empty.

- It's extremely rare for people to be bitten and die from a cone shell bite, but it has happened.

You use a stick in front of you to check for creepy-crawlies on the forest floor, but in fact you don't need to worry too much: there are very few small creatures here that can hurt you, at least not seriously.

The island becomes quite steep as you move towards the centre, and it's hard going in the heat. At least you're shielded from the hot sun by the canopy of trees above you.

You suddenly get the feeling you're being watched . . . you hear a sound, and freeze, looking around you warily. Goosebumps prickle on your skin as you listen. There it was again! You swallow hard. Maybe there's someone there? You call 'hello'. Your voice sounds small and quavery, but loud enough for whatever is there to hear you. There's no reply. The sound seemed to come from over to your left, through some dense foliage. Maybe you should go and investigate?

If you decide to investigate, go to page 108.

If you decide to ignore it and keep going, go to page 105.

You lean out of the raft and aim the flare well away from it, making sure your back is to the wind, just in case sparks from the flare touch the raft and sink it. You take off the flare's cover and fire. The flare goes whizzing up into the hazy dawn sky, burning bright red. It burns for about a minute. Surely the ship must see it.

You wait expectantly for the ship to slow down and change course. But nothing happens. The ship doesn't change speed or direction, but sails quickly through the sea, away from you. You watch it until it's a speck on the horizon.

Many of the large ships that sail the open seas don't have lookouts. Everyone on board was probably asleep.

Go to page 113.

You're woken by the dawn light and open the zip on your raft for a look out. Who knows what you'll find – maybe a desert island, or a cruise ship, or a pod of friendly dolphins who'll guide you to shore.

Sadly, there's nothing like that. But there's a rain of small splashes on the calm sea in the distance. They come closer as you watch – flying fish, skipping across the ocean towards you.

Soon you spot something else: it looks like a large metal box, and you're heading straight for it. It's a shipping container, floating at the moment though it'll eventually sink. Should you let the raft blow towards the container, to see what's inside it? It might be something useful. Or should you paddle away from it, in case it harms the raft somehow?

If you decide to paddle away from the container, go to page 88.

If you decide to investigate the container, go to page 92.

Flying Fish

- Flying fish are common in warm seas all over the world. There are 40 or so different types, the biggest measuring up to about 45 centimetres long.

- Underwater, flying fish gather enough speed to break the surface – up to about 60 kilometres per hour. Then they spread their fins, which act like wings to carry them through the air.

- Flying fish can glide over a metre above the surface of the sea, and can cover 200 metres in one glide.

- Flying fish are attracted to light, and fishermen use a light at night to catch them. Even when no one's trying to catch them, flying fish sometimes end up inside boats!

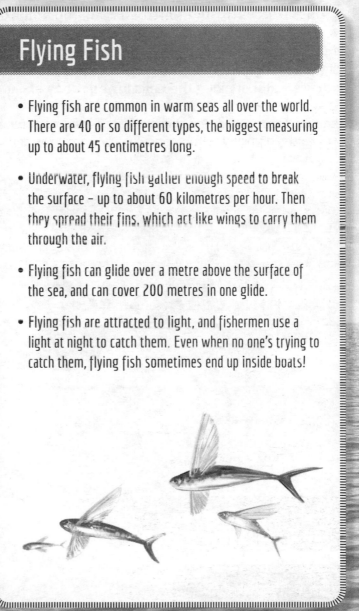

The raft is encrusted with sea salt. You collect a small handful and eat some. Soon you start to feel better. If you hadn't done this it might have led to hyponatraemia – where your body is unable to process water, making the cells in your body expand.

The wind has dropped almost completely. For the first time, the raft isn't pitching and rolling on choppy waves. You drift along slowly in the current.

Go to page 104.

Hyponatraemia

- Without enough salt, people can develop hyponatraemia, a low level of salt in the blood.

- If you drink a lot of water without eating any salt to replace the salt lost from your body by sweating, or from vomiting or diarrhoea, you could be at risk of hyponatraemia. It can also be caused by major organ failure.

- The body's cells swell up with water if there isn't enough salt. When brain cells swell it's especially dangerous because the skull limits how much the brain can expand, causing it to press on the skull.

- Symptoms of hyponatraemia include headache, confusion, tiredness, nausea, muscle spasms and seizures.

- In severe cases, hyponatraemia can be fatal.

You're jolted awake. It's the middle of the night, and you can't see a thing. What woke you?

There it was again! A bump underneath the raft. Should you try and find out what's causing it? Or go back to sleep and forget about it?

If you decide to investigate, go to page 78.

If you decide to go back to sleep, go to page 28.

Sailing at Night

- Solo sailors have to sleep, but unlike you they have radar and proximity sensors to alert them if they're likely to crash into something in the dark.

- Even with electronic equipment, sailors have to keep watch during the night if they're sailing in a shipping lane, or if they're close to land.

- Ships have navigation lights so that another ship can see which way they're heading – and whether they're on a collision course!

- On a clear night far from land, you will see many more stars than anywhere other than the most remote places on land. In the past, sailors used them to navigate.

- You might be lucky and see phosphorescence in the sea, caused by marine animals and plants that glow naturally at night.

The snakes are indeed venomous, and you were right to get away from them (even though you would have to try quite hard to get them to bite you – see page 69 for more information).

You spot several fish that look as though they'd make a good meal. But you know that there are some poisonous fish that live in tropical reefs and lagoons. Which of these fish should you spear and eat?

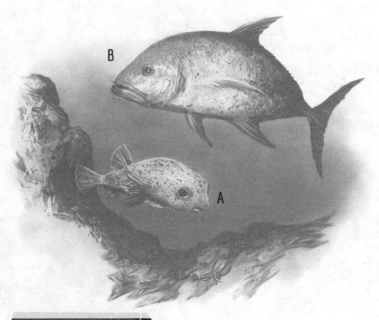

If you spear fish A, go to page 66.

If you spear fish B, go to page 75.

You haven't chosen well. The pool is a haven for mosquitoes, which are attracted to the smell of your blood in the night and feast on you hungrily while you're asleep.

Go to page 84.

You reckon that if you eat just one of the red, pea-like seeds, you'll be OK even if the plant is poisonous. If you get an upset stomach in a few hours' time, you'll know not to eat any more of the seeds. You take a seed, crunch it between your teeth and swallow it.

Unfortunately for you, this plant is very poisonous. Even one seed is enough to kill you, if the seed's protective coating is broken. After a few hours, you start vomiting and have diarrhoea . . . and it gets worse from there. You are badly dehydrated, and drink from your water container. But it's not enough to save you. After a couple of days your major organs stop working, and you die.

The end.

Rosary Pea

- The rosary pea, scientific name *Abrus precatorius*, is a type of vine native to Africa, Asia, Australia and parts of the South Pacific. It's known as the rosary pea and also the jewellery plant, because the brightly coloured seeds are sometimes used as rosary beads, or in jewellery – though this isn't recommended because of the poison the seeds contain.

- The plant's flowers are small and white to pale pink or lavender. After flowering, the plant forms seed pods that split open, revealing the brightly coloured seeds inside. They're usually bright red with a black cap.

- The seeds contain the toxin abrin. The rosary pea is one of the most poisonous plants in the world.

Behind the beach, the forest rises up in a gentle slope that becomes steeper. Maybe you should search in the forest, where there are lots of trees and low-growing plants to choose from. On the other hand, it's dark in there, and there might be snakes or spiders or other creepy crawlies lurking on the forest floor.

If you decide to search for fruit trees along the beach, go to page 100.

If you decide to look inland, go to page 112.

South Pacific Fruit

- Breadfruit is part of the staple diet of the South Pacific – it's a good source of starch, and tastes similar to bread or potatoes when it's cooked. It grows on large evergreen trees, and looks like a bumpy melon. You might not have seen it because it doesn't keep well, so it's not exported very often.

- Coconut palms are common. The liquid inside a coconut is sterile as well as tasty – it can even be used in surgical procedures.

- Bananas were (probably) first domesticated in the South Pacific, on the island of New Guinea, around 10,000 years ago. Today there are hundreds of different varieties. Bunches of bananas don't hang down, as you might expect, they point upwards.

- Other tropical fruit you might find includes guavas, papayas and passionfruit.

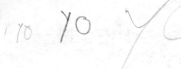

You manage to spear the fish, and triumphantly take it back to the beach and the embers of your fire. You feed the fire, roast the fish on a stick, and tuck in.

You caught the fish completely by surprise, spearing it before it had even caught sight of you. If it had felt threatened, it might have puffed itself up into a ball, so that the spines on its skin stuck out – which might have made you realise that this is a poisonous pufferfish.

When you're eating the fish, you notice a tingling sensation on your lips and tongue. The poison works quickly: you feel dizzy, weak and sick, and within minutes you're lying paralysed on the sand. A few minutes later, you're dead.

The end.

Pufferfish

- There are lots of different kinds of pufferfish (also known as blowfish), and not all of them are poisonous. But pufferfish include some of the most poisonous animals in the world.

- Some pufferfish only grow to about 2.5 centimetres long, while the biggest kind, which lives in freshwater, can measure up to about 60 centimetres.

- The fish have elastic stomachs that allow them to blow up into a ball several times their usual size.

- The poison contained in pufferfish is tetrodotoxin, which works on the nervous system, and is deadly. There's enough poison in a pufferfish to kill 30 adult humans.

- In Japan, pufferfish is an expensive delicacy, prepared by specially trained chefs who know how to remove the poisonous parts of the fish.

- Some pufferfish are brightly coloured to show other creatures that they're poisonous, while others are camouflaged.

- Pufferfish prey on small shellfish and fish. The bigger kinds can crack open hard shells with their tough beaks.

You are sure you spotted a fish disappearing into these rocks – you feel around inside the rock crevices, and feel a sharp nip. You whip your hand away. Suddenly you feel something on your foot – one of the black-and-white snakes sinking its fangs into you!

You were right to think that sea snakes aren't usually dangerous. The snakes are venomous – very venomous, in fact – but they rarely bite because they are shy creatures. Also they have short fangs that don't inject very much venom. Unfortunately, though, you have threatened them by poking your hands into the rocks where they were hiding, and you have been bitten twice.

You get back to shore before the venom starts to act, but once it does, it's lethal.

The end.

Banded Sea Krait

- Banded sea kraits live throughout the tropical waters of the South Pacific and Asia, particularly around islands. They can measure up to 1.5 metres long.

- Their venom is ten times more powerful than a rattlesnake's, but they rarely bite humans, and don't inject much venom when they do. When people are bitten, it's usually because sea kraits have become entangled in fishing nets.

- The banded sea krait's powerful venom is used to catch fish and eels – the krait isn't as fast a swimmer as its prey, so it needs a fast-acting venom to stop the prey escaping.

- The creatures can stay underwater for up to two hours, but need to surface to breathe air. The banded sea krait is unique among sea snakes because it spends some of its time on land, where it goes to mate, lay eggs, and digest food.

You're in luck – the beach is sandy, and it's easy to jump out into shallow water and drag your raft up onto the sand behind you. Dry land! If you weren't completely exhausted you'd do a little dance to celebrate.

You haul the raft further up the beach and decide to make a camp and investigate in the morning. You find the waterproof bag with dry clothes and blankets, change your wet clothes for dry ones, wrap yourself in the blanket and fall asleep.

The sound of birdsong wakes you at dawn. The beach is made of fine, silvery coloured sand. You're in a small cove, surrounded by rocks. You decide that the first thing to do is make a shelter. You find a large shallow pool by the rocks on one side of the beach – maybe that would be a good place for your shelter. Or maybe you should build your shelter near the trees, at the edge of the beach?

If you decide to build your shelter near the pool, go to page 61.

If you decide to build it at the forest edge, go to page 89.

Shelter Building

- The site of your shelter is extremely important. It needs to be on flat ground, away from animal trails, not on an exposed site, and not somewhere that's prone to flooding, or where biting insects live.

- Unless you have a desalinator, you'll need to find a source of drinking water, and it makes sense to build your shelter near to your water source.

- Caves make good long-term shelters – they're ready-made, and all you need to do is build a covering for the entrance. But check that the cave isn't already inhabited by a wild animal, and for the possibility of rock falls. Unfortunately, there aren't any caves on your beach.

- In a tropical climate, try to raise your shelter off the ground, away from ants, centipedes, spiders and scorpions.

- If you're feeling up to it and there are plenty of fallen logs around, you could try building a log cabin. Lay your first layer of logs in a square or rectangle, then cut joints into the tops of the logs for the next layer to fit into. Make a roof from broad, waxy leaves.

You were right not to eat the plant: in fact it was a rosary pea, which is very poisonous – just one seed could kill you (see page 63). You do need to eat some fresh fruit or vegetables, though. So you carry on looking.

Go to page 102.

You remove the cap and fire the flare, which makes a spectacular blazing arc high into the sky. For good measure, you take the other one and fire that too. Now the ship is bound to see you.

You wait expectantly. The ship continues on its way, showing no sign that it's seen you. You gaze out at the ship as it sails past. How could no one have seen your flare? But the ship is quite a long way away now, and someone would have to have been looking in the right direction to have seen the flares. You've been unlucky.

Unfortunately, you don't have any flares for when you see another ship. Muttering curses, you throw the flare case onto the sand.

 Go to page 100.

You take the paddle and make a big splash in the sea, then turn it over so you're holding the paddle end and stab downwards into the water with the handle. You're hoping the sharks will see this as a threat, and swim away.

It doesn't seem to be working, though. If anything the sharks look as though they're circling closer to the raft.

Go to page 18.

You manage to spear the fish, and triumphantly take it back to the beach and the embers of your fire. You feed the fire, roast the fish on a stick, and tuck in.

You've caught a jackfish, and it tastes delicious. It's just as well you didn't catch the other kind (see page 66). Your jackfish was fine but sometimes eating certain kinds of larger fish caught on reefs, such as barracuda, grouper and snapper, can give you ciguatera poisoning: symptoms include stomach pain, vomiting and diarrhoea, and it can last for weeks though most people recover over time. Though they're usually fine to eat, the fish, which aren't usually poisonous, can carry the poisoning from eating contaminated seaweed. You might be better off sticking to a vegetarian diet from now on.

Go to page 96.

Y ou rub your eyes, because you can hardly believe what you're seeing. You squint into the distance again: it's a ship! And it's coming your way! You're going to be rescued!

But first you have to make the ship see you. Although your raft is bright orange, it's small. You need to do something to make sure the ship sees you.

In your survival pack you find some distress flares. One of those should do the trick – but, on the other hand, the burning flare could damage your raft and sink it. You could signal with the mirror, honk the horn and blow the whistle – the ship is on course to pass quite close to you. What should you do?

If you decide to use a distress flare, go to page 53.

If you decide to shout and wave, go to page 99.

Shipping Lanes

Shipping lanes are established routes for commercial ships that criss-cross the world's seas.

- The Dover Strait, in the English Channel between England and France, is the world's busiest shipping lane. Around 500 ships per day pass along the route, which makes it hazardous for smaller boats . . . and cross Channel swimmers.

- Another extremely busy shipping lane runs along the Malacca Straits, between the island of Sumatra and Malaysia and southern Thailand, connecting the Indian Ocean with the South China Sea. Shipping in the Malacca Straits is sometimes targeted by pirates – there are around 20 cases a year.

- Shipping lanes aren't nearly so busy in the South Pacific, but shipping sails along trade routes bound for international destinations, including remote Pacific islands.

You unzip the raft and look out. The sea is fairly calm, the sky is scattered with millions of stars, and there's a bright moon, almost full. You scan the sea for signs of life, desperately hoping you don't see a dorsal fin cutting through the sea towards you. You can't see anything – in fact the bumps were made by bottlenose dolphins, but they've swum away.

As you look across the calm sea, you're met with the best sight you could possibly have imagined: land! It must be an island – maybe even an inhabited one. You're quite close – close enough to paddle to it – and in the moonlight you can make out a narrow strip of silvery sand. You grab the paddle and get moving.

Go to page 70.

Pacific Islands

- South Pacific islands are scattered across tens of thousands of kilometres. People first colonised them many thousands of years ago – see page 116 for more on the first Pacific Islanders.

- The many islands of the South Pacific are divided into Micronesia, Melanesia and Polynesia, but even within those geographic areas, cultures and landscapes can differ widely. Find out about the biggest and smallest South Pacific islands on page 9.

- There are lots of other island groups in the Pacific Ocean. The Galapagos Islands, hundreds of kilometres off the coast of South America in the Pacific, are home to unique animal species. The Philippines, the islands of Indonesia, Taiwan and other Chinese islands, and the islands of Japan, are all in the Pacific. Much further north, the Aleutian Islands are a chain of small islands that separate the Pacific from the Bering Sea – most of them are part of Alaska.

You do have to take care in this part of the world – there are lots of different dangerous sea creatures lurking where you least expect to find them. Added to that worry, some of the fish that live on reefs and in lagoons are poisonous – even fish that aren't usually poisonous, depending on what they've been eating in the reef (see also page 75).

You've been very unlucky, because among the rocks and sand just next to the shoreline there's a perfectly camouflaged stonefish. A terrible pain shoots into your foot as spines on the stonefish's back pierce into it. The stonefish's venom is extremely powerful, and your foot swells very quickly. You collapse on the sand, in agonising pain, unable to move. Within a couple of hours, you're dead.

The end.

Stonefish

- Stonefish are the world's most venomous fish. They live in shallow waters and coral reefs of tropical coasts.

- Their lumpy, stone-coloured bodies look almost exactly the same as the rocks they live among.

- Stonefish venom is carried in the fish's spines along its back, which it raises when threatened.

- The venom is strong and works quickly, but you have a good chance of survival if only some of the spines have penetrated your foot, or if the spines haven't pierced the foot deeply.

- Stonefish can live out of water for up to 12 hours. People have trodden on them walking along the beach at low tide, metres away from the sea.

- Stonefish are also known as goblinfish and warty ghouls.

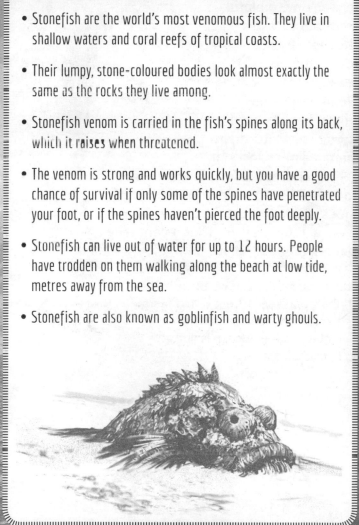

You have to be a pretty good climber to make it up a coconut tree – there aren't any helpful branches to use as foot holds. You remember seeing a TV programme in which people used a strong scarf to help them climb coconut palms, and you take off your T-shirt and use that to help you. Your deck shoes slip, and it takes ages to get even a little way up, but eventually you get the hang of it.

Unfortunately, you get five or six metres off the ground when your T-shirt tears on the bark of the tree, and you plummet to the ground, bashing your head on a rock.

The end.

You sharpen a stick to use as a spear and swim out to the rocks. The water's calm and clear, and you can see little fish darting all around you. You take a deep breath and dive under the water. There are lots of brightly coloured fish here, most of them too small to bother with, but you spot some bigger ones swimming in and around the rocks.

As you get closer to the rocks, your breath almost running out, a white-and-black striped sea snake flashes past you. There's another one disappearing into the rocks. You surface to take a breath.

You are pretty sure that sea snakes aren't dangerous. Should you ignore them and carry on hunting for fish in the rocks?

If you decide to hunt in the rocks, go to page 68.

If you decide to swim away from the sea snakes, go to page 60.

It really wasn't a very good idea to build your shelter right next to this pool. Some of these mosquitoes carry malaria, and you've been bitten by one.

You feel fine for about ten days, surviving on the island quite happily and feeling confident of rescue. But then you start to feel sick: you get a pounding headache, a high temperature, and flu symptoms. After a few more days you start to vomit and have diarrhoea. The flu-like symptoms continue.

It takes a while, but the parasites that cause malaria have set up home inside you. Your body does its best to fight them, but with no medical help, you die.

The end.

Malaria

- Only a female anopheles mosquito can carry malaria. The disease is caused by the plasmodium parasite, which gets into the bloodstream via the mosquito's bite. There are four types of plasmodium parasite but only one of them causes malignant malaria – there's another type of malaria, which isn't deadly.

- Symptoms usually appear between about ten days and four weeks after you've been bitten, but sometimes people don't get any symptoms for up to a year.

- As long as you are diagnosed with malaria early enough and take medicine, malaria probably won't kill you.

- If you come from a country that doesn't have malaria-carrying mosquitoes, you're more at risk because you won't have built up immunity to the disease.

- Over a million people die from malaria every year, mostly in Africa, because they aren't treated in time.

- Mosquitoes carry other diseases too, such as yellow fever and dengue fever, which can also be fatal.

You use the paddle to move the raft closer to one of the floating things. As you dip your hand into the water, you feel a terrible pain – you've been badly stung! You cry out in pain, drop the creature back into the water, and grab your arm.

You've been stung by a Portuguese man-of-war, which look a bit like jellyfish but aren't. They have a sting like a jellyfish's, though, and it's extremely painful. You writhe about in agony, wondering if the sting is fatal. It starts to feel a bit better and you wash the sting – which has left bright red marks on your arm – in salt water, keeping well away from the rest of the creatures.

You doze for the rest of the day, on and off. The wind picks up, and the jellyfish-like animals are blown away. After a long snooze you wake up to find it's night-time. You take a look out of the raft, and forget about the pain in your throbbing arm instantly – there's an island! You start paddling for it.

Go to page 70.

Portuguese Man-of-War

- Portuguese man-of-wars, also known as bluebottles, aren't jellyfish, but floating colonies of closely-related creatures, which can't survive alone. The colony floats from a bluish-coloured gas-filled bladder, trailing venomous tentacles deep into the water – the tentacles can be as long as 50 metres.

- They get their name from a Portuguese sailing ship – the floating bladders look a bit like a ship's sail (if you squint a bit).

- The creatures are carnivores, and use the tentacles to catch their prey – usually fish.

- They can't move on their own, but are blown along by the wind or moved on ocean currents.

- The man-of-war's venom can be very painful to humans, and in very rare cases it can kill if the victim has an allergic reaction to the sting.

- Loggerhead turtles eat Portuguese man-of-wars, along with jellyfish. The turtles' tough skin is too thick for the venom to penetrate.

It's hard to paddle the raft – the wind and the current make much more difference to where it's heading than you with your paddle. But you manage to avoid the container, which is leaking a cargo of flip-flops into the sea. You're glad you decided to paddle, because you can see a jagged metal edge that could easily have spelt your doom.

Go to page 76.

You spread out your raft on the beach, secured with stones, so that it dries out in the sun, and search the forest edge for a good spot to make a shelter.

You find a bent tree that looks like a perfect spot. You drag some fallen logs out of the forest, using a stick to check the forest floor for creepy-crawlies. Then you prop them up against the bent tree to make a lean-to shelter. You spread the raft material over it to make it waterproof, and secure it with large rocks so that the material won't blow away. You find some broad leaves to go on the floor of the shelter, then spread your dry blankets out on the floor. You move all your other supplies into the shelter, feeling very pleased with your handiwork.

Go to page 98.

There's nothing wrong with eating insects, as long as you know which kind you're eating. Since there are poisonous kinds of almost every type of insect, you were foolish to eat the crickets without knowing for sure that they're an edible kind. But luckily the crickets you've caught and squished are not poisonous. You roast them over your fire, and they provide a tasty and nutritious source of protein.

But you can't live on crickets alone if you're going to survive on this island for a while. You need fruit and vegetables as well, otherwise you might end up with scurvy – a horrible disease that's caused by lack of vitamin C. You spot a likely looking plant: its dried seed pods are filled with tasty looking bright red and black seeds.

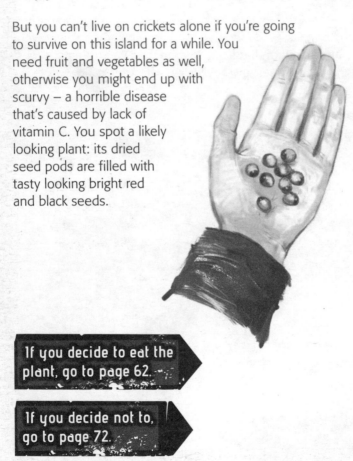

If you decide to eat the plant, go to page 62.

If you decide not to, go to page 72.

Eating Insects

- Lots of people around the world eat insects as part of their daily diet, and have done for thousands of years. Insect eating is widespread in Central and South America, Africa and Asia.

- Some of the more popular insects are crickets, grasshoppers and ants, as well as scorpions and tarantula spiders (which are both arachnids rather than insects). Sometimes it's the grub stage of the insect that's eaten.

- Eating insects is an ecological way to get your protein – no fields need to be cleared to graze cattle, for example.

- Insects and arachnids are types of arthropod. Shellfish are in the same family group, yet people in Europe and North America tend to be squeamish about eating land-dwelling arthropods, but don't mind eating arthropods that live in the sea.

The raft floats towards the container, which is huge close up, and is spilling out thousands of pairs of flip-flops into the sea. As you get closer, you realise the container has rusty, jagged metal edges, and try to paddle away from it. But it's too late: you're too close, and a gust of wind blows the raft up against the container and tears it.

The raft sinks quickly. You hang on to the container, but you don't last long.

The end.

Pacific Plastic

- Rubbish in the sea, especially plastic, causes damage to sea life, ensnaring fish and marine mammals and killing turtles, which mistake floating plastic carrier bags for jellyfish, and eat them.

- Because of the way the ocean's currents move, a lot of the rubbish from all over the world ends up in the Great Pacific Garbage Patch, mostly in the form of tiny pieces of plastic.

- There's an Eastern and Western section of the Garbage Patch: the Eastern patch floats between Hawaii and the United States, and the western patch floats between Hawaii and Japan. They're connected by a current more than 9,000 kilometres long, where more rubbish floats.

- 90% of the garbage patch is plastic.

You run downhill as fast as you can, leaping over fallen logs and rocks, pushing aside creepers, your heart pounding. You have to get down to the beach and signal to the ship!

You fall over, scratching yourself on a thorny plant, but get up and dust yourself off before plunging onwards to the beach. When you finally get there, you're completely out of breath. You put your hands on your knees and pant, at the same time scanning the sea for the ship.

It's there – but quite a long way away now. Is it worth sending a distress flare?

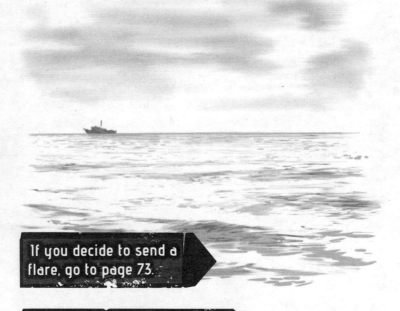

If you decide to send a flare, go to page 73.

If you decide not to, and wait for another ship, go to page 47.

You're eating breakfast one morning – bananas again – when something makes you look up. You're not sure, but you think you can see a ship – though it's very far away. Unless it's your mind playing tricks . . .

An hour later, and it's definitely a ship! You try not to get too excited – maybe the ship won't come any closer. Even if it does, maybe it won't see your distress flares. You get the flares out of your shelter and read the instructions so you'll be ready when the ship's within range.

The ship still seems to be heading your way, but it looks like it's starting to change course. You think it's close enough to spot your flare but you're not sure. You decide to send a flare anyway. You fire it high into the sky in the direction of the ship.

You stare at the ship, willing it to change direction . . .

Go to page 114.

There don't seem to be any people living on the island, but you haven't explored it yet – there could be a village on the other side for all you know. Some uninhabited islands in the South Pacific have holiday homes for tourists who want to experience life on a desert island. Even if there aren't any signs of life, you decide, it would be silly not to explore it.

The island rises steeply in the middle – it's probably an ancient volcano. From the top of the thickly forested hill you'll get a good view of the whole island. You set off, taking a bottle of water with you.

Go to page 52.

Volcanic Islands

- A volcano is a split in the Earth's crust where hot molten magma from deep inside the Earth can erupt. Volcanic islands are formed when undersea volcanoes erupt over a long period of time, growing in size until they break the surface of the sea to form an island.

- The Hawaiian Islands are a chain of volcanic islands caused by a hot spot under one of the plates that forms the Earth's crust. As the Earth's plate moves over the sea bed, over millions of years, it moves the old volcano with it, and a new volcanic island is created over the hot spot. In Hawaii, the oldest island is a volcano millions of years old that's no longer active. In the distant future, new volcanic islands will probably form in the chain.

- The Galapagos Islands were also formed in this way, and so were the islands of Japan. In 2013 a new volcanic island popped up in the Pacific off the coast of Japan.

- Volcanic islands are also known as high islands. There are lots in the South Pacific, some with volcanoes that are still active.

You might be here for a while. The shelter looks good, and your water needs are sorted, whether you find a source of freshwater or not, because of your desalinator. That just leaves food.

You start to have a look around and notice some rock pools on one side of the beach. Inside are some cone-shaped shells a bit longer than your hand. They look as though they might have creatures inside them that might be good to eat. Should you pick one up and find out? It would certainly be a very easy meal.

If you decide to try one of the shellfish, go to page 50.

If you decide not to and to make a fire instead, go to page 40.

You wait until the ship is at its closest point, then stand at the open flap of your raft waving your T-shirt in the air wildly, honking your horn, blowing your whistle, and screaming for all you're worth. You can't see anyone on board, but you keep making noise and waving anyway. The ship is surprisingly noisy as it churns past you. It shows no sign of slowing down.

Now you wonder whether it would have been better to risk sending a flare. (Actually, it wouldn't have – there's no one on lookout on the ship to see you or a flare anyway.) You watch the ship sail off into the distance, towards land, hot food and soft beds. You can't help imagining how different it must be to be on the ship instead of in this tiny raft. You feel more helpless and alone than ever.

Go to page 113.

You've got used to fishing and collecting fruit to survive. You've spent time making improvements to your shelter, and it's now more like a treehouse, on stilts to keep you away from the ants, spiders and other creepy-crawlies that sometimes crawl out of the forest. You don't often go into the forest, and every time you do you make a careful search of the horizon for ships. You use rocks to spell out SOS in enormous letters on the beach, in case of a passing plane or helicopter.

After a few weeks you do see another ship. You don't have a flares left, but you make a smoky fire, and jump up and down on the beach shouting and waving. The ship doesn't see you.

You survive for several months on the island, but in the end, even without a distress flare, you're rescued. A small plane spots your SOS, and sends a rescue helicopter. Soon you're looking forward to seeing your family and friends again. You are overjoyed when the pilot tells you that your uncle was found by fishermen only a day after the storm that washed him overboard.

The end.

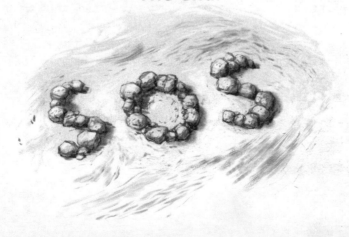

Some of the trees along the beach are palms – they look like coconut palms. You search on the ground for fallen coconuts, but can't find any. The trees are tall, and swaying in the breeze, but you think you can see coconuts at the top. Maybe you should climb one of the palms and gather some?

If you decide to climb a palm tree, go to page 82.

If you decide to look for fruit somewhere else, go to page 112.

You'll need to find plants to eat somewhere. You know that if you don't eat fresh fruit or vegetables, or find some other source of vitamin C, you'll get scurvy – a horrible disease that makes your gums bleed and your teeth drop out and eventually kills you. You shudder at the thought.

You've spotted some seaweed – maybe you could eat that? Or maybe you should explore a bit further and see if you can find an edible plant somewhere else?

If you decide to eat some seaweed, go to page 106.

If you decide to look for something else, go to page 64.

The climb becomes steeper, and you're puffing and panting as you reach the top. You climb up on to bare rock, above the tree line. There's a crater in the centre of the island – this must once have been a volcano, but it doesn't look as though it's erupted recently. You turn and look out across the island.

The island is a circle of green in a turquoise sea. You can see the silver sand beach and cove where you've made your shelter. Rocks surround the rest of the island, which is covered in dense forest. It's beautiful, but there is no sign of life.

Close to the island the water's light blue, becoming darker as the water deepens. As you scan the sea further from the island, you spot something that makes your heart pound: it's a ship! You have to get back to the beach before it passes by!

Go to page 94.

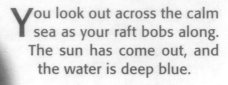

Y ou look out across the calm
sea as your raft bobs along.
The sun has come out, and
the water is deep blue.

You spot something in the
distance. You can't work
out what on Earth it might
be – it looks like a flotilla of
blue plastic, and you're heading
straight for it . . . soon you're in the midst of dozens of weird-
looking transparent floating bags. Underneath them, long
fronds reach down into the water.

Should you hook one with your
paddle, and take a closer
look? Maybe it's
edible. On the
other hand, perhaps
these strange things
are dangerous.

If you decide to take a
closer look, go to page 86.

If you decide to leave them
alone, go to page 110.

You continue uphill towards the centre of the island. You still feel as though someone – or something – is watching you, and you're seriously spooked for a while. But nothing happens. Maybe it was some kind of harmless animal.

Go to page 103.

You gather some of the seaweed. It doesn't look that appetising, but it's an easy way of getting your greens. You've heard that seaweed is a common food in the South Pacific, and you can see why – there's lots of it.

You clean the seaweed and try a bit raw. It tastes OK, but you decide to boil it up in some water over your fire. You like it a bit better that way.

Although seaweed is indeed eaten in the South Pacific, you were unwise to eat some without knowing for sure that it's an edible kind – some types of seaweed can upset your stomach, which is the last thing you need in a survival situation.

It might be good to find some fish to go with your seaweed.

Go to page 83.

Edible Seaweed

- Seaweed is an important part of the South Pacific diet – it's eaten in Fiji and other South Pacific islands.

- Several different kinds of seaweed are collected from shallow lagoons and reefs, mainly by women and girls. The seaweed is harvested from different areas in a cycle of a few weeks, so that it can grow back ready for the next harvest.

- Different types of seaweed are eaten in different ways, some cooked and some eaten raw, with different flavourings including lemon juice and chili.

- Seaweed is eaten in lots of other parts of the world too: laver is a type of seaweed eaten in China, Japan, Korea and Wales, where it's made into laverbread.

You look up, and almost scream with fright: about 25 pairs of eyes are staring at you from a tree about two metres away!

They are huge, furry bats, hanging upside down from branches, with their leathery wings wrapped around them. Most of them are asleep, but some have opened their eyes and are staring at you with interest. Now that you've got over the initial shock, they look very cute, with beautiful big brown eyes. You don't go any nearer – you don't want to alarm them. But you watch them for a bit before you head back uphill, towards the centre of the island, leaving the bats to get back to sleep.

Go to page 103.

Fruit Bats

- Fruit bats are also known as flying foxes or megabats, and include the world's largest bats. There are lots of different kinds – the biggest have a wingspan of up to 1.7 metres. But the smallest kind is only six centimetres long, which is smaller than some other kinds of bat.

- On some South Pacific islands, fruit bats (and sometimes other smaller bat species) are the only native land mammal.

- As the name suggests, fruit bats eat fruit, and some eat nectar from flowers. On some Pacific islands they're seen as a pest and hunted.

- These large bats don't use echolocation as other bats do. Instead they use a highly developed sense of smell, and large eyes that are adapted to see in twilight and dark forests. There's an exception: the Egyptian fruit bat does use echolocation.

- The bats are also hunted for food in the South Pacific – apparently they taste delicious.

- Fruit bats have been known to carry viruses that are fatal to humans, though the bats don't get sick themselves, so it's just as well you didn't get too close.

You watch the floating things warily for signs that they might harm you or the raft in some way, but they just drift along in the current. They don't seem as though they're aware of you being there at all. These creatures are known as Portuguese man-of-wars (find out more about them on page 87), and they sting, so it's just as well you didn't touch one.

Soon the wind picks up and you lose sight of the strange creatures. You sleep on and off for the rest of the day and into the night. You wake up and look out of your raft: the sky is studded with stars and you open the canopy, lay back and watch them for a while . . . when you hear what sounds like surf breaking on a beach! You jump up and look out – there's an island not far away! You start to paddle as fast as you can towards the beach.

Go to page 70.

You drink some water from the bottle in the Grab Bag. But you don't feel any better – if anything you feel worse. Soon, you feel dizzy and confused, and lie down.

Low levels of salt in your body have led to hyponatraemia (see page 57) – your body is unable to process water without salt, and the cells in your body are expanding. You're feeling dizzy because the cells in your brain are expanding.

You fall into a coma and die.

The end.

It's not long before you find a fruit you definitely recognise – bananas. Some of the fruit is yellow and ripe, and you eat it hungrily. It tastes delicious.

Bananas contain vitamin C, though they aren't as good a source of it as oranges and other types of citrus fruit. But you should get enough of it to ward off scurvy.

Go to page 96.

You feel awful. And it's not just because of the rapidly disappearing ship. You have a thumping headache, and you feel weak and tired. You wonder if it might be a good idea to drink some more water? Or maybe you should find some salt to eat? You know that low levels of salt in the body is just as dangerous as not enough water to drink especially when you've been sweating.

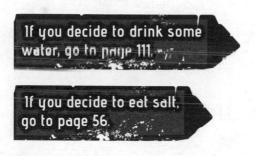

If you decide to drink some water, go to page 111.

If you decide to eat salt, go to page 56.

Your heart is pounding as you wait desperately for the ship to turn – and it does!

It's a cruise ship, full of happy holiday makers. It makes an unscheduled stop close to your island. By this time, you're jumping up and down, waving, and crying with relief. Some of the crew get into a dinghy and sail across the shallower water to your beach. You ask the crew about your uncle, and discover some good news – he was found by fishermen only a day after the storm that washed him overboard! Relieved, you're soon looking forward to a meal, a comfortable bed and seeing your family and friends again.

You're safe at last!

The end.

People of the South Pacific

People crossed thousands of miles of open sea to discover the remote South Pacific islands. They came by canoe, navigating by the stars, 1,700 years before European or Chinese explorers managed to make long sea voyages. They settled on islands scattered over 30,000 square kilometres of the Pacific Ocean, and different cultures grew up on the different island groups.

People first colonised the Pacific islands around 50,000 years ago, arriving in New Guinea from Asia and the Indonesian islands. The first South Pacific long-distance sea-farers are known as the Lapita. They travelled from New Guinea to colonise islands further east more than 3,000 years ago. They sailed with nothing to help them navigate apart from the stars, yet they managed to bring people, animals, farming equipment and plants across the vast Pacific. They first colonised the Solomon Islands, then moved on to the Santa Cruz Islands, more than 350 kilometres to the east. Fiji, across another 800 kilometres of empty ocean, was colonised next. Eventually, between 300 and 900 AD, people spread all the way to Hawaii, the Cook Islands, Easter Island and New Zealand.

The Pacific islands were colonised by Europeans, like most of the rest of the world, from the 1500s. Today most islands are independent, apart from a few that still belong to the United States, France, Chile and New Zealand.

Real-life Lost at Sea Stories

Adrift in a Life Raft

Poon Lim holds the record for lost-at-sea survival. He survived 133 days on a lifeboat in the South Pacific in 1942-43, after the British merchant ship he worked on was torpedoed and sank during the Second World War. He survived for a couple of hours in the sea wearing a life jacket, then boarded a life boat he found drifting. There were some supplies in the boat, and Poon Lim also caught fish (including a small shark) and seabirds, and collected rainwater. He was finally rescued close to land by some Brazilian fishermen.

William and Simonne Butler survived 66 days adrift in a small life raft in the Pacific Ocean after their yacht was attacked by a group of pilot whales and sank, in June 1989. They drifted hundreds of miles towards the coast of Costa Rica, where they were eventually rescued, having survived by catching and eating fish and turtles. They also had a desalinator, without which they might not have survived.

Steve Callahan was sailing his yacht across the Atlantic single-handed in 1982 when it collided with a whale and sank. He abandoned ship and took to his life raft, and was rescued by fishermen within sight of land 76 days later. He had eight pints of water and two solar stills, and, like the Butlers and Poon Lim, he survived on fish and seabirds. Also like them, Steve Callaghan spotted various different ships on the open sea, none of which saw him.

Paul Lucas didn't even have a life raft! In 2000 he was diving off the coast of Australia when he drifted too far out in stormy seas. He spent 24 hours floating in his wetsuit, then spotted an island and swam to it. He was rescued soon afterwards.

Desert Island Survivors

In 1722, **Philip Ashton** was captured by pirates. When they stopped at the uninhabited Roatan Island, off the coast of Honduras, Ashton escaped and hid in the jungle until the pirates left. He survived on the island for over a year before he was rescued, in 1724.

It was **Tom Neale's** dream to live on a desert island. In 1952, he was left on Suwarrow atoll in the Cook Islands, where he lived happily all alone. He left the island because of illness, but returned from 1960 to 1963, and again for a final ten-year stay from 1967 to 1977, when he died

Glossary

barnacles shellfish that attach themselves to rocks or other underwater surfaces

buoyant able to float

canister cylinder-shaped container

colonised land taken control of by people from another country

condenses changes into liquid

contaminated unclean

dehydrated suffering from a lack of water

dorsal towards the back

echolocation using the echoes of calls to work out how far away objects are

embers hot, glowing coals that remain at the end of a fire

harpoon long, spear-like instrument

hyponatraemia lack of salt in the blood

hypothermia dangerously low body temperature

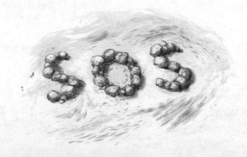

kindling small, dry twigs used for lighting a fire that will burn quickly and easily

lagoon shallow body of water separated from larger body of water by islands or reefs

listing leaning

parasite creature that lives in or on another creature

phosphorescence light generated by marine animals and plants

pod group of dolphins

scurvy deadly disease caused by a lack of vitamin C

sterile free from germs

submerged under water

tinder very dry material that is easy to set on fire

torpedo weapon that propels itself under water towards its target

toxin poisonous substance

venomous capable of injecting venom (poison)

Index

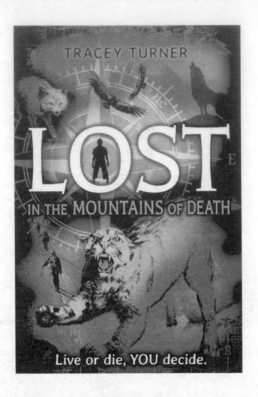

Lost… In the Mountains of Death

You've survived the vast and perilous Pacific Ocean, but have you got what it takes to survive the freezing temperatures and deadly heights of the Andes Mountains? From deadly blizzards to hidden crevasses, can you make it out alive?

With unexpected threats hidden around every corner and the risk of hypothermia ever present, will you be able to make your way to safety and avoid the deadly perils of the Andes Mountains?

Live or die – you decide.

£4.99   ISBN 9781472906212

Extract from Lost... In the Mountains of Death

Slowly and carefully, you walk towards the rocks where you thought you heard the noise. As you round a large boulder, you find out what caused it. You are staring into the yellow eyes of a large puma.

You feel sweat break out on your forehead and swallow hard. The animal is big and muscular. It hasn't taken its eyes off you and its ears are flattened against its head. You figure that this probably isn't a good sign. In fact it's difficult to see anything good about this situation. The puma is only a few metres away from you – just a couple of large bounds of its powerful legs and it would be on top of you.

What should you do?

If you decide to curl into a ball and play dead, go to page 38.

If you decide to back off, go to page 27.